W9-CQF-905

Make A Wish Bear

by Greg Foley

SCHOLASTIC INC.

May your wish come true

Early one evening, a little bear
made a wish on a little star.

Bear sat and sat,
but nothing happened.

Mouse found Bear sitting alone.
"What are you doing?" she asked.
"I'm waiting for my wish to
come true," said Bear.

Mouse sat down to wait.

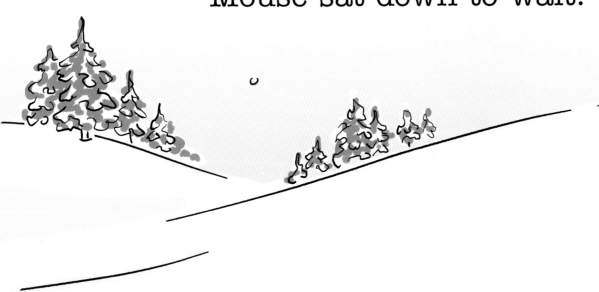

Soon Owl came by.
"We're waiting for Bear's wish
to come true," said Mouse.

"For a wish to come true," said Owl,
"you can't say it out loud."
"I didn't say it out loud," said Bear.
"Shhh," said Owl.

Then Fox walked up.
"We're waiting for Bear's wish
to come true," said Mouse.

"First you must close your eyes," said Fox.
So Bear closed his eyes.
"Cover them," said Fox.

Not long after, Elephant arrived.
"We're waiting for Bear's wish
to come true," said Mouse.

Elephant said,
"Try standing on one foot."
Everyone tried standing on one foot.

Pretty soon Turtle came along
and said, "If you hold your breath,
maybe it will come true."

"For how long?" asked Bear.

Then Bunny hopped up.
"What are you all doing?" he asked.

Bear looked around.
"If a wish already came true,"
he asked, "can you say it out loud?"

"Of course!" said Mouse.
"What was your wish?"

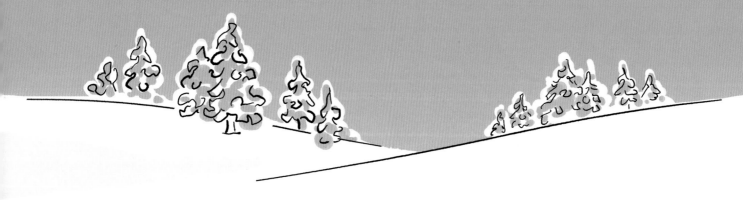

"To be together with all of you!"

No part of this publication may be reproduced, stored in a retrieval
system, or transmitted in any form or by any means, electronic, mechanical,
photocopying, recording, or otherwise, without written permission of the publisher.
For information regarding permission, write to Viking, a division of
Penguin Young Readers Group, a member of Penguin Group (USA) Inc.,
345 Hudson Street, New York, NY 10014.

ISBN 978-0-545-51534-4

Copyright © 2012 by Greg Foley.
All rights reserved. Published by Scholastic Inc.,
557 Broadway, New York, NY 10012,
by arrangement with Viking,
a division of Penguin Young Readers Group,
a member of Penguin Group (USA) Inc.
SCHOLASTIC and associated logos are trademarks
and/or registered trademarks of Scholastic Inc.

12 11 10 9 8 7 6 5 4 3 2 1   12 13 14 15 16 17/0

Printed in Malaysia   108

First Scholastic printing, December 2012

Set in American Typewriter Regular
The line art and color for this book were
digitally rendered from pencil sketches.